FASHIONISTA

For Mali and Maya

First US edition 2022
First published by Hachette Australia 2019

Library of Congress Catalog Card Number 2022930501
ISBN 978-1-5362-2377-4

CCP 27 26 25 24 23 22
10 9 8 7 6 5 4 3 2 1

Printed in Shenzhen, Guangdong, China

This book was typeset in Helvetica and Franklin Gothic.
The illustrations were done in watercolor pencil and collage.

Candlewick Press
99 Dover Street
Somerville, Massachusetts 02144

www.candlewick.com

FASHIONISTA
FASHION YOUR FEELINGS

written and illustrated by
MAXINE BENEBA CLARKE

CANDLEWICK PRESS

Some dress-days are

MUD-STOMPING

don't-care-what-you-wear.

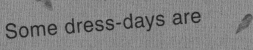

You

PUDDLE- SPLISH

in worn-out kicks

with

BED-RUMPLED

hair.

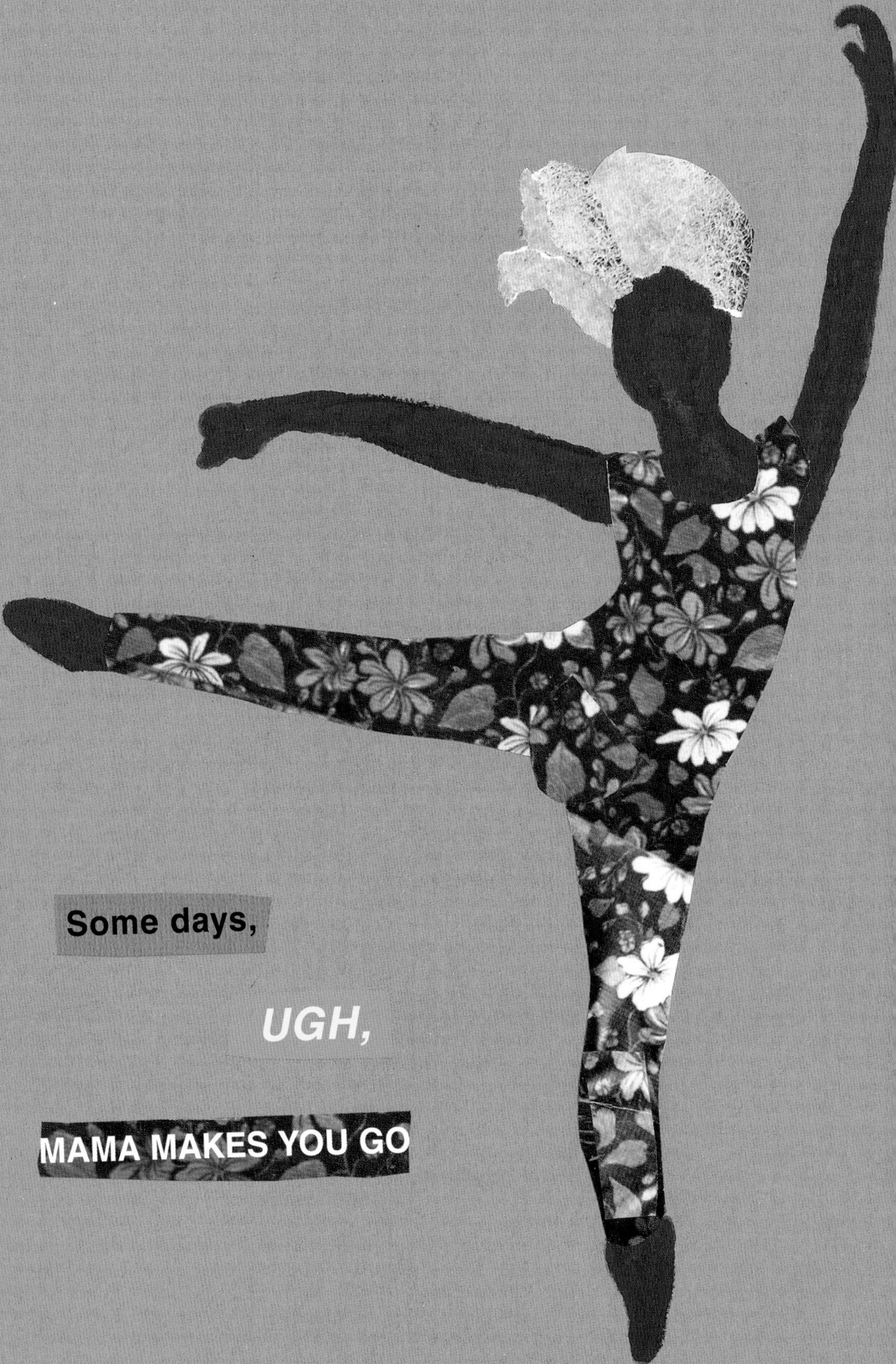

Some days,

UGH,

MAMA MAKES YOU GO

BROTHER - MATCH - SISTER.

But on other days . . .

BOOM.

Strut it.

You're a

FASHIONISTA!

A fashionista
digs fashion.
That means they
think it's cool fun

to **DRESS UP,**

STEP OUT,

and

SHOW OFF

looks they love.

Be your

BOLD - BIG - SELF,

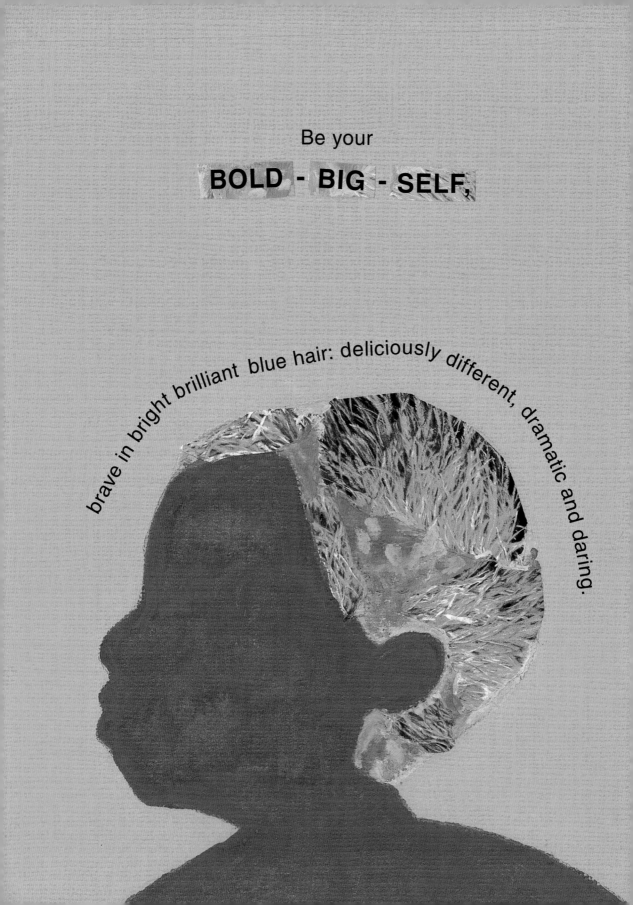

brave in bright brilliant blue hair: deliciously different, dramatic and daring.

Rock a **RUBY-RED** dress.

Let them *know*
you're a
QUEEN.

ROYAL

RUFFLE-

PUFF-

PUFFLED,

right

down

to

the

seams.

Tap dapper in
a jacket,
fancy suit, or

BOW TIE.

Is this you
waltzing by, looking

MIGHTY-
BIG-FINE?

Put on your **PASSION.**

WE COULD ALL BE FEMINISTS

Wear your HEART on your sleeve.

YOU'RE A

FASHIONISTA!

Work it.

Rock it.

BELIEVE.

Some dozy days are
who-cares-what-you-wear.

You stay
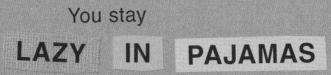 **LAZY IN PAJAMAS**

and don't comb your hair.

You're a whatever-mess
of **CRIMP-CRUMPLE
AND CURL,**

and you
so-what
don't-care
about the
FASHION
WORLD.

Some days are
can't-be-bothered,

COMFY - CARELESS,

JUST-BLEND-IN.

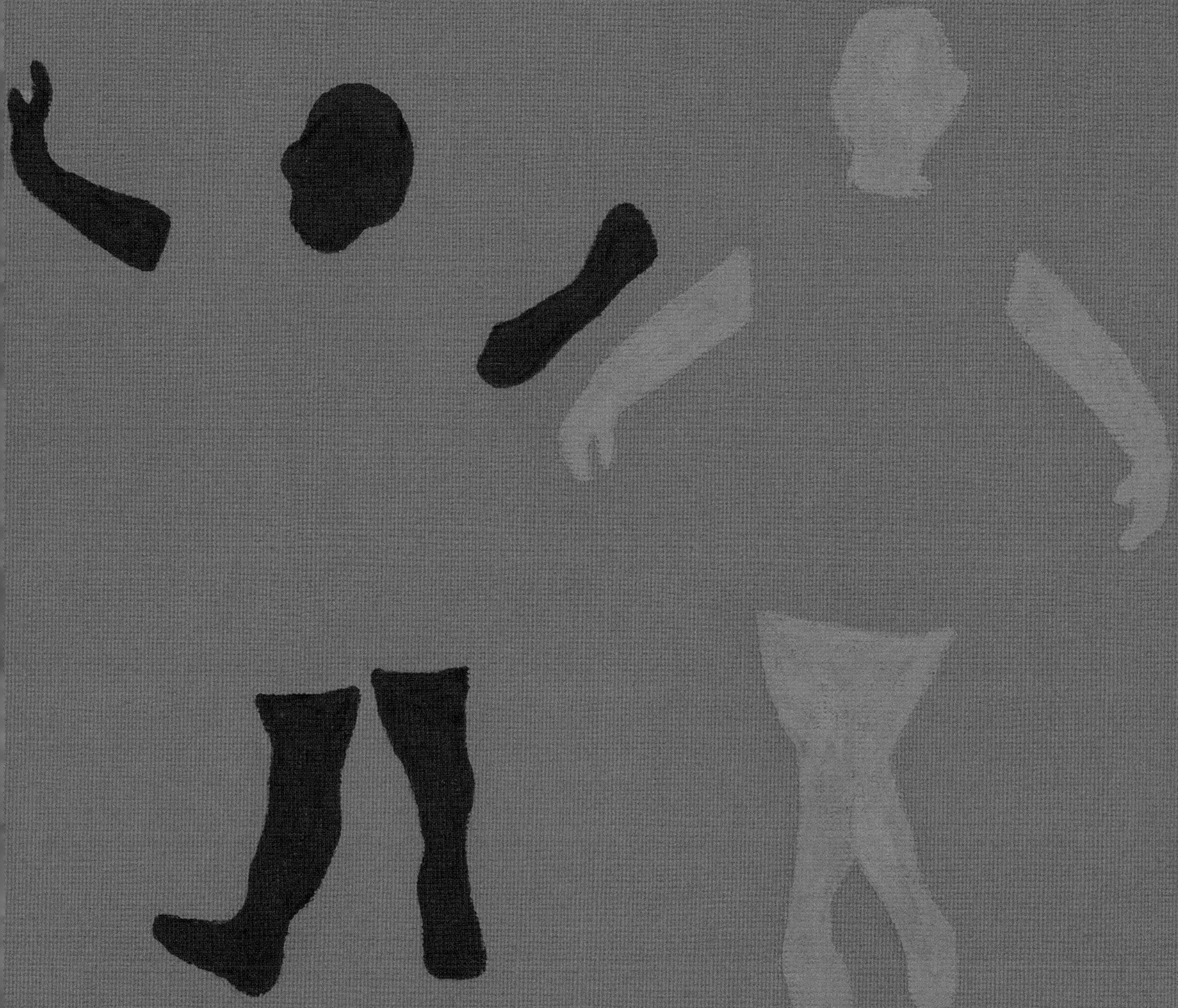

But on
other days . . .

CHIC-
A-
BAM!

You're the fashion
KING!

So pretty-proud-prance
in your

HOT POP

PINK

LEGGINGS:

fox-trotting,
toe-tapping,
and
quirky quickstepping.

Be particular about

PATTERNS.

Save up all your

STRIPES,

and kookily-carefully

long-layer all the lines.

Knee-high
brown boots
can be
favorites
for
weekends.

Tuck your

DENIM

JEANS

in so the whole street

can see them.

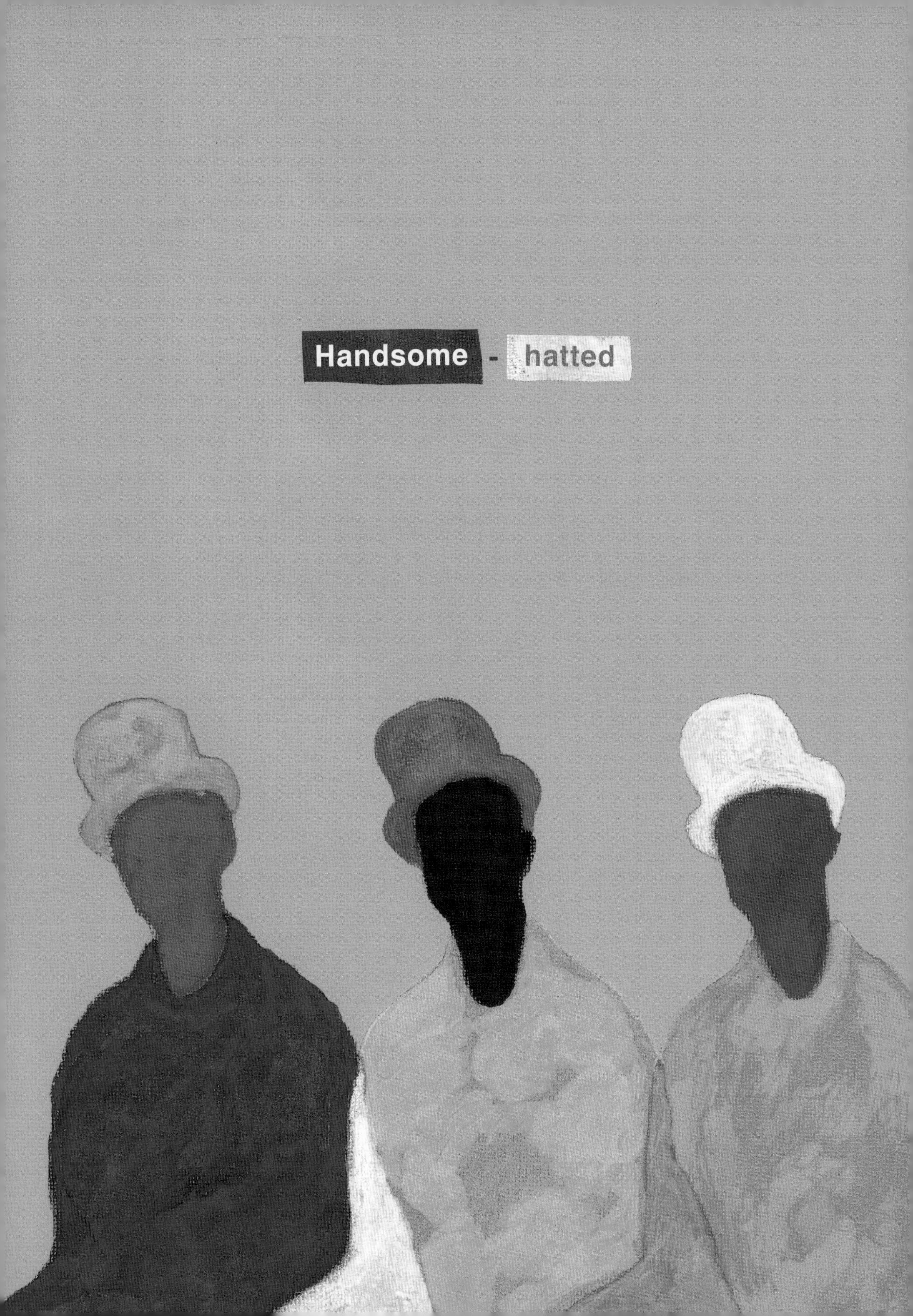
Handsome - hatted

in high-harmony,

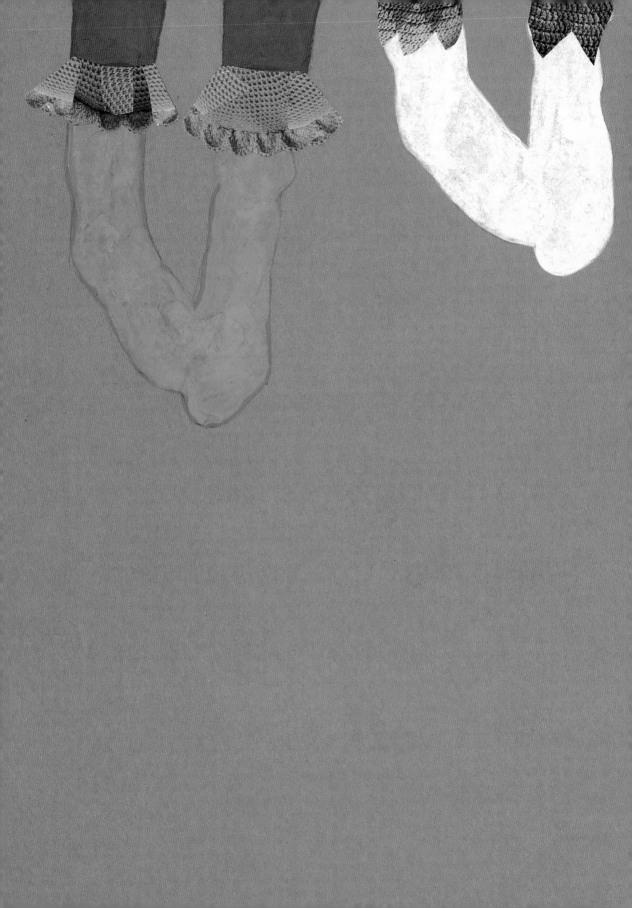

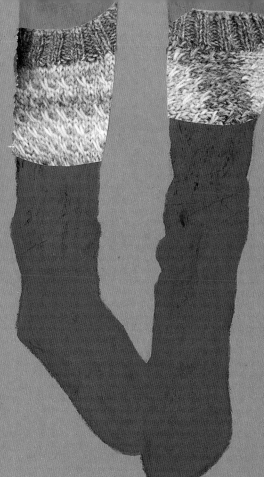

or

SILLY - **BILLY**

in socks.

With an
elegant

AFRO

or clipped,

COLORED

locks.

Low-down loan
Mama's lipstick.
Let it
SHIMMERY-
SHINE:

SPARKLY
SPECIAL,
and delightfully
divine.

Fancy-frolic in **FEATHERS**, if that makes you grin.

Find something you **LOVE,** and fast-make it your thing.

Wear your

wardrobe

however:

HOMEMADE,
hand-me-down,

or BRAND-NEW.

Fashion your

FEELINGS:

SHOUT IT

loud-roaring-big,

or sing shy-like-a-whisper:

"CHIC-A-BOOM!

CHIC-A-BAM!

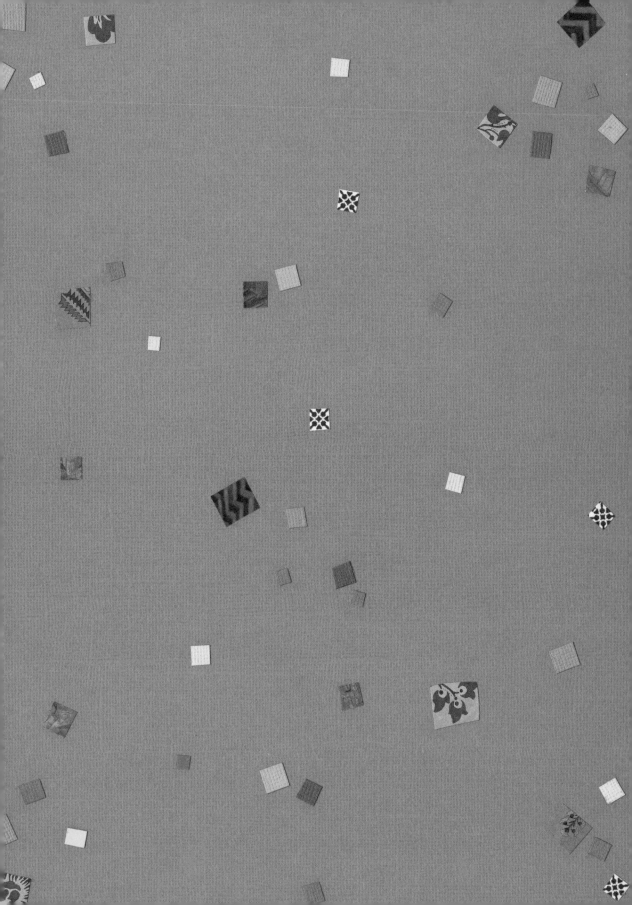